The Selkirk Seven

Melanie McCurdie

Copyright © 2016 Melanie McCurdie
Cover Model: Jessika Dillard
Photo by Danny Calling Chase
MorbidX Alternative Modeling
All rights reserved.
IBSN-13: 978-0995152502
ISBN-10: 0995152500
melaniemccurdie.com

The Selkirk Seven

This is a work of fiction. Names, characters, businesses, places, events and incidents are either the products of the author's imagination or used in a fictitious manner. Any resemblance to actual persons, living or dead, or actual events is purely coincidental.

No part of this book, be it digital or hardcopy, may be reproduced or transmitted in any form or by any means, electronic or mechanical, including photocopying, recording or by any information storage and retrieval system, without written permission from the author

DEDICATION

For my boys

Sam and Davey

I love you both

Table of Contents

A Prelude to a Nightmare	1
A Ghost Story	3
Selkirk Keep	14
The White Haired Vulture	21
The Dark Sparks	28
Voices Behind The Door	39
Hidden Dangers	45
Death and Elinor's Madness	56
History's Hollow Game	65
Miracle Eyes	81
A Book of the Dead	95
My Legacy	99
The Way It Ended	115

ACKNOWLEDGMENTS

My cup of gratitude runneth over.

Thank you to my lovely cover model, Jessicka Dillard of Morbid X Alternative Modeling and her talented photographer and husband Danny Calling Chase xoxo

GREETINGS!!

BEFORE YOU BEGIN, A FEW DISCRETIONARY WORDS:

KEEP OUT OF REACH OF CHILDREN

Everything written from this point forward is to be considered snippets from my own twisted imagination and/or my own opinion.

The words (the) follow are not an official representation of any human, animal (warm blooded or cold blooded), extradimensional beings and/or biologically challenged individuals.

Actual offences or nightmares may vary from individual to individual. If conditions persist, stop reading. Some reassembly may be required. Batteries and weapons not included. Objects in mirror *are* closer than they appear.

Gratitude does not include tax, title, license or freedom from further subjection to bloodsauce.

Enjoy your read.

An idea, like a ghost, must be spoken to a little before it will explain itself.

Charles Dickens

A Prelude to a Nightmare

The story you are about to read is a work of fiction and of fact. For the sake of my own mind, I prefer to think it as just that, as story, a work of fiction. It took many long days and nights of long hard thought and at the peril of my own sanity to come to the decision to publish my experiences. It is only through the undying love and encouragement of those cherished few that the words finally were able to break free. I have fought to hold onto the belief that it is was all my imagination. Over the past year, during those times when I was at my lowest and so full of regret, that belief is all that I had left to hold on to.

To this day, no one can shake me of it, least of all myself. No matter how often I try to pretend that it was simply an overlong nightmare, the delusion does not hold. People I loved and cared for lost their lives, and in ways that I personally never imagined could happen outside of a movie theatre or book. It happened. For those that still doubt the veracity of my claims, surely the photographs that were published in the national newspapers and gossip mags of my injuries prove the extent of my wounds.

Very often, I hear the impatient tone behind the sympathy and the words, "but you survived!" I lived, but did I survive? Do the few examples in the pages that follow give proof of life or proof of existence enough to satisfy? That is your decision to make.

My name is Moira Tavist and this is my story.

A Ghost Story

FEBRUARY 13, 2014

Winter had been long and it seemed that our biologically challenged planemates were in rare form. I could barely keep up with the requests for us to investigate locations that were suspected to be haunted. Not that I'm complaining. That would be like starving to death at a buffet. The only thing we were suffering for was enough investigators for all the requests.

Three weeks ago, while I was researching one of our upcoming adventures, I came across a contest that was taking place on one of the local news stations and naturally I entered.

That was when I first (because) acquainted with Selkirk Keep. I knew that the assorted nuts that I worked with would probably kill their own mothers to win the chance to visit such a darkly historic location just to tour it, let alone spend the night. Obviously it's an exaggeration, but you get the idea. I wasn't so sure I wanted to go, but I also knew I'd be talked into it and so I decided to let them convince me. Besides, to the victors go the spoils, so they say, and this was quite a coup should we win the chance.

Selkirk Keep was completed in 1535, after being commissioned by King Culen of Selkirk. The castle had been investigated only once, about three and a half years ago and that one time resulted in its closure to any and all public traffic. Odd enough to pique my interest and quite sufficient enough for the crew to be hooked through their twisted little hearts.

It seemed to be in remarkably good shape for such an old building, and it was currently privately owned. The soft ping of my phone that announces that I have email distracts me from the mindless surfing and the ceaseless chatter of the bodily challenged. An unfortunate hazard in my line of work is that I am never truly alone. It is also a secret joy of mine, to know this. Some would consider it a double edged sword, and they would be correct, though voicing such a thought isn't something I would do. I'd never live it down.

Through the wonders of modern technology, and strangely so, considering that Selkirk Keep had been in the forefront of my thoughts as of late, the email brings good news for the team. It's also news that makes my guts cramp, and comes in the form of a congratulatory eLetter. A sure sign of change on the wind.

"Selkirk Keep calls you home!" proclaims the first line and it turns my spine to ice. There is something about that line that is sending the other dimensional beings around me into a tizzy. Perhaps I need to rethink my decision to be convinced. Every little girl dreams of living in a castle with her Prince by her side but this particular stone edifice is enough to make me want to vanish. Laughing to myself over the ridiculousness of that thought, I text the ragtag bunch of fiends I called friends to tell them to assemble and then began to do some preliminary research into a location that Eric Dupree, the team leader, booked that had sent the team into raptures with morbid delight.

Happy Valley Rest Home. It sounds like some kind of Merrie Melodies cartoon to me, but it turns out to be an abandoned mental hospital – fabulous – and it was reportedly haunted - even better. To top it all off, we had been given free run of the place. Now I was afraid.

There was also another from the television station with the press packet and the legal paperwork that was required. There was an attachment that intrigued me far more. It contained more interesting information about Selkirk Keep, including photographs. Such a wealth of discovery that I was now privy to. My heart throbs with anxiety, because although I am absolutely positive my fiends would cum in or out of their pants over either, they will definitely take Selkirk over all other opportunities. It is crude and I know it, but you had to know them. It is absolutely apt.

My phone starts chiming moments before the bells above the front door announce the arrival of said fiends. Loud and snarky, all, they burst into my office like bad tempered dust devils, landing wherever they did, and each with glare in my general direction. I know they hate it when I demand their presence without explanation, but it's the only way to get them all here at the same time.

"Ever heard of Happy Valley Rest Home?" I drop the name on them in a rare lull in conversation to the expected snorts of laughter and inappropriate gestures. Jake Jepson, our newest member snickers like a teenager, and I can just guess there is some story behind it. Eric shakes his head, and sips his coffee while he waits. As I expected, one grave, wide-eyed stare brings a smile to my cheeks. Ah, one of them *is* paying attention although it isn't who I expected.

"This isn't about Happy Valley, Moira. What are you up to?" Logan Roofe's tone is suspicious and nervous; a combination that is eerily familiar to me and one I've never heard from him. The expression he wears banishes it from my mind, however, and I instead focus on the wary response. There is information being withheld here and I wonder how he knew that I was keeping information about Selkirk Keep under my hat.

This certainly wasn't the kind of thing that could be released to the public past the words "under suspicious circumstances." I know that nothing more has ever said about it.

"You're right Logan. I entered us into a contest on Wellsprings TV a few weeks ago, on a lark. We won. The prize is two weeks, all expenses paid, carte blanche while on location at Selkirk Keep, including full equipment, and we maintain film rights. *And...*" Now that I had their full, undivided and for once, I paused and waited. There was a voice whispering in my ear about bloodlines and loyal practices that was informative and becoming increasingly disturbing.

"And *what,* Moira? *What* could be worth going there? Do you know anything about that place? The stuff that happened there...." Logan stumbles over his words then glowers exasperated in my direction. Smiling, and nod my head in agreement.

Of course I know, but I wonder how much he does and how since it is purported that there were no survivors from the last team. Hence the closing of the site.

I can't get a read on Logan, and its strange when he has always been an open door. A flurry of activity and voices invades the blessed silence, shattering it like the glass in the kitchen that Charley dropped in the kitchen, adding her quite inventive curses to the mix. No one can ever say that we are a boring bunch. Dragging a chair over in front of my tense colleague, I sit then lean forward with my elbows on my knees. He flinches back when I touch his wrist, shocked at how cold his skin feels, and reply," Yes Logan. I know almost everything. There is only one thing that I can't understand. How do *you* know? It's as yet unreleased information." Quietly, and clearly I speak only to him. He really is terrified and it shows. "Logan, how did you get away?"

Admittedly, the last question was thrown in without hopes of getting an answer. I'd be more likely to get a chair across the back of the head as a word from him at all, after that. He surprises me by turning his earnest and incredibly young face to me and in the same tone I used with him, tells me how he got away, and why he'd said nothing about it. His reasoning makes perfect sense, and still, I bully him into coming along when he really wants to run out the door. I really want to join him.

Jodee Dean and Mark Conrad are back, bickering back and forth as they always have. This time the discussion ends with her sucking suggestively on her finger and smirking at me around it. "Cut your finger Jodee? I knew you were a fucking vampire." The sound of raucous laughter breaks the spell; even Logan snickers along with the rest and the room sighs relief.

Back on track, Eric and I answer their questions for a good hour, armed with whatever information we had gathered, and then shooed them out the door with orders to take the next day off. They needed to rest, focus and I had some things to do that didn't require an audience observing my every move.

That included Eric, whom, once we were alone, I kissed as thought it had been eons since we touched and sent him along too, with the promise of more, later.

Long live the internet, I easily found what I needed and then some. It took remarkably less time to complete a task that I had expected to be difficult in no time, and would be home before I expected to my delight. Of course, life never goes that way, does it? As I was leaving and fiddling with my keys, a light and movement from the equipment room catches my attention. I peek around the doorway, and spot Logan nervously fiddling with something on the desk in front of him.

It was too easy and I cleared my throat just to watch him jump then sigh. "Why must you do that every time Moira? Why don't I sense you every time, right?" He laughs but it sounds strained and a little vague. "Caught you!! What are you doing here? I thought you ran for freedom like the others," I giggle madly.

Logan turns with several pieces of equipment in his hands, and snorts, "I thought we could use this stuff. It all still works and this one," he holds up his left hand, "has footage I haven't watched from last investigation. Maybe it's time – what do you say Moira? His usually handsome face contorts into something resembling a death mask for a moment and then blinks out of sight, and he smiles shyly, "Want to watch a movie with me?"

SELKIRK KEEP

JUNE 29, 2014

There it stands, Selkirk Keep. It's thick stone walls are dirty and stained from centuries of Mother Nature's wrath, and still a lovely building. The Fiend Team is nearby, all of them huddled and murmuring their excitement at entering this long forbidden fortress. I'm not excited at all, not after too many hours on a plane and the ensuing sea of humanity that we had to wade through. Or the long, cramped and exhausting drive only to wait over an hour late for our benefactor.

The night is chilly and the damp of the English countryside does not help my otherwise anxious disposition. Any reservations I may have had about this place as the time for departure drew closer the misgivings have now become so much more. The land is seeded in darkness; there are too many echoes of the past here, too many spirits and some of them aren't really dead. They only believe that they are. I can hear their voices playing off the inner walls, still immersed in their own daily grind of living and dying.

From down the long, winding driveway, a pair of headlights stab the dark, spooking deer and the other more sinister nocturnal creatures that roam freely on the grounds. Our benefactor, it seems, has finally had the good graces to arrive. Eric shoots me a silent warning when I open my mouth to remark on the less than polite behaviour of this individual and I bite my tongue with a sigh.

Even in the dark, the grounds are lush and green, very well-manicured and beautiful gardens sprawl here and there, the very type that one has come to expect from this part of the world. The breath of thousands of flowers hangs in the air, and their perfume is almost cloying in its sweetness. It all makes this challenge seem so much more surreal. Jodee smiles widely when she catches me rolling my eyes at her excitement. Granted, it is a lovely spot but it somehow feels like camouflage.

From a white Bentley steps a tall man with a large fringe of frizzy blond hair and crooked teeth, all smiles and good cheer. *Lovely, he's late, I'm freezing and he's smiling like a -* Given some face paint he would resemble some creepy clown from an old timey film. Eric's finger is raised and pointed in my direction, a not quite order to behave myself. Apparently my efforts at honing my poker face are failing miserably.

Still, here we are, and it was my tenacious tendencies that have brought us here in the first place. I may as well enjoy it while we wait for the negotiations to conclude. There has been no evidence of spirits that has caught my attention since our arrival. There is, however, a frequency whine in my ears that is ill at home with my environment. As soon as it arrived, the noise is gone and the discussion behind me is nothing more than white noise as I take in my home for the next two weeks.

Selkirk Keep was completed in 1535, according to the information and my own net-stalking, fact-finding expeditions by King Calum of Selkirk for his wife, Queen Elinor. The castle is a marvel of construction, each stone fits perfectly with the next, even after all this time. The walls are only slightly off kilter, and the view is awe inspiring. Above our heads, the window ledges are straight and wide enough to sit on and take in the scenery and still remain relatively safe.

From an upper walkway, a lantern burns, and the flames make shadows puppets on the walls that resemble daemons dancing. I wonder who lit the lanterns when there is no one inside the building, which is why we were waiting. I glance at our benefactor, Mr. James who is trying to convince Eric of something and, Eric, shouting in a frustrated way, throwing his hands in the air almost comically. Oops, trouble in paradise, I suspect Leaving them too it, I wander a little closer to the massive wooden door that leads into the castle proper. I'd guess it to be approximately 15 feet tall and at least that wide. It reminds me of the movies about medieval times, like something not quite Hollywood. Impulsively, I reach out my hand to touch its scarred surface and the past jolts through me as though I am on fire.

The stink of blood and corruption fills the air. My sinuses burn and my head rings with the bellows and groans of men in various stages of injury.

There are horses everywhere, close enough touch, and their breath is white in the air. It must be winter. Everything is same, and then I am different. The world is spinning – there is a woman peering out at me from the castle walkway, her dark hair loose on her shoulders and blowing in the breeze - she leans over and too far. She should be falling but is instead floating and is beaming directly at me. Her eyes are strong, insistent - her arm reaches out, her finger beckons, inviting me home -.
"Yes, I will. Thank you."

There is movement behind me, and I jolt just before Logan's hand lands on my shoulder. "Moira? Are you okay?" His question is lost among the other voices far in off, almost lost the din. "There is a woman here, Logan. I still see her, as though she's been imprinted on my brain. She looked directly at me. That's never happened before. Do you know who she is?"

I stammer, shaking my head. It hadn't, not with this kind of premonition, but it isn't a premonition, it is closer to a memory. The English language lacks an apt description of the sensation, frustrating me further. I'm fighting the urge to run as far and fast as I can and from the expression on Logan's face, he is thinking the same thing. "I don't want to be here, Moira. Can't we leave?" All I can do is pat his shoulder and shake my head. My friends are loaded down with equipment and excitedly chattering away. So it is settled then. We are going in and I am positively terrified.

After tonight, nothing will be the same again. I know it.

THE WHITE HAIRED VULTURE

No one else can see him, the apparition in the entryway, judging from the lack of startled reactions. He is lurking in the corner, almost indistinct in the daytime shadows, and watching the goings on with interest. This man is dressed in livery and rather ornate at that, and I can only assume he was a servant of some sort, certainly he belongs to the building. He simply watches my friends with a malevolent smirk on his rotting lips, bare eyes flicking from one to the next of the people I care for with a calculating countenance. It makes me angry for no reason at all, a killing rage that invades wholly.

Never could have I imagined anything close to the heinous violations I was being forced to witness behind my eyes. What kind of person would perform such horrid acts and expect me to visit these same on each and every living being in this place? Each vision is worse than the next, and they are making me both ill, and aroused. As violently as I am able, I shove as hard as I can inside myself to rid the abominations I had been assaulted with from my brain. The apparition that had been observing us earlier was now openly gawping with a deranged expression that was enough to make me recoil. What the hell is haunting this place?

He smiles, and I feel faint, then vomitus. This is what I am up against? We've barely begun to unload the equipment and already I feel we are all in serious danger. I won't survive this, and the team - I can't save them if I can't save myself

There's a buzzing, an eye watering pitch in my ears - it's so close and clap my hands to my head to shut it out but it's no use, it just gets louder, from a mosquito whine into words. My name? Eric's appears, his hands on my arms shaking me slightly. His actions only partially cut the hold the evil thing in the corner has on me. I can't seem to get it through to him that we have to leave, and he. is speaking words that I can't hear over the too loud buzzing. "Eric? I'm cold. Are we inside yet? What is that noise?"

Everyone is staring at me. There is no air to inhale and I'm suffocating. In a panic, and pulling free from his grasp, I break for the door. There is no way in Metistopheles' unholy vacation spot am I going to stay here one more second. The door won't open no matter how hard I yank on the handle. "Why won't it open? I need out of here."

I can hear my voice harsh in my ears, as harsh as rushing and wheezing laugh from that nasty creature hiding in the shadows. Desperation turns into full-blown panic at finding my escape blocked. A great bellow of laughter rings in the foyer where we are setting up home base, and my grey matter screams in unison with the maniacal glee in that voice. The only way to stay sane is to bang my head as hard as I can on the strong wood of the door. The grip loosens as the bright white stars grow brighter with each thud. The Devil has his hand on my back and it burns my like acid. I have to twist away, try to run but He has me held fast in his molten grip. "Moira, do you hear me?"

I look up to see the pall of Eric's normally robust complexion turning his concerned face, worrisome; the way his mouth pulls down in a frown mars his normally cheerful and handsome face. "Eric?" I begin to cry when he nods and holds me close to his chest.

Eric, we can't stay here. I won't stay here, please don't make me stay," I babble at him, my hand twisted in his damp t-shirt.

"What did you see?" he asks me quietly, and I feel his muscles flex with the motion of the over the shoulder to take in the rest of the team. He tilts my chin up so that I have no choice but to meet his eyes and the horror there is more than I can stand. Thick blood begins flowing from his eyes, nose and ears. It is staining the crisp white collar of his button up shirt and drooling over the hand that is still entangled there. He whispers my name, asks again what I saw, and pieces of his shredded tongue bounce off of my arm to fall at our feet. They resemble small pink erasers, like the ones on the end of a pencil, just bigger. I shake my head, and back away, willing my hand to unclench the grasp I have on him. Closing my eyes against the unspeakable message I am being given is doing little to help and I suppose that is the intended purpose.

It's very obvious that whatever still resides here intends to cause us harm, and I am being forbidden to ruin its fun. Eric reaches out to grab my arm to halt my efforts to escape, and pulls me back so that I am against him with his ruined mouth at my ear to whisper, "it's not real. I'm fine, open your eyes and see for yourself. Whatever it showed you is a lie." I can't help it and shudder against his gore soaked shirt, then do as he asks with my heart in my throat.

The same old Eric I've known forever without a cut or a streak of blood and the same crooked smile with the scarred upper lip from where I'd punched him after a late night dare. I stagger in relief against him and observe my friends. Bless them, they are attempting to look busy while connecting computers, monitors and cameras. JP is untangling recording equipment wiring and muttering in an undertone that I am positive are cuss words.

"This place will be wired for sound and they will hear nothing, Eric, *nothing!*" but all he does is shush my efforts and stroke my back in an admittedly soothing manner. I sense someone else too close, and shake my head against the interruption, reburying my face in his chest. "Moira," Charley Fargo insists, in that tone I know all too well murmurs at my shoulder, "I saw it too. Heard it. But listen, it's not your concern. We all knew what we were coming into, the risks involved. We all made our choices to be here."

I can't believe what I am hearing. I *know* that they chose to be here, we all did but to own the knowledge that they may die and go on anyway? I didn't agree to that, and I won't agree to lose them. I lift my head from Eric's chest and step out of his embrace to think about where we stood. We won this opportunity, a real chance to prove our talents and show the world the truth. Is it worth our lives?

They stand loosely grouped together, the team, watching us gravely. Appraising Charley, who still stands at my side, I see the truth in her eyes. They know what's here, they choose to stay anyway. If anyone gets out of here alive, it'll be a blue-eyed miracle

THE DARK SPARKS

I still hear that laugh in my head and it makes my stomach roll over. There is no way that I can unsee Eric's bleeding face, or those horrible images that were forced into my head. *Maybe if I close my eyes for just a few minutes*

"Moira? Moira, wake up! Can someone find a cold cloth or something?" The world is black and that is just fine, in fact it would be perfect except for the muffled thudding in my ears. Except for the voice very close to me. My body feels chilled yet I can feel that I am laying on something warm and I turn my head to bury my face in its comfort, feeling tears slide from my eyes.

Crying is not my favourite expression and I seem to be doing it an awful lot since our arrival. The scent is familiar, one that makes me want to burrow in and recoil in self-preservation. Eric. "I want to go home." It's a fact. I want to go home and never step foot from it again. I try to move and feel his arms tighten on my body, holding me in place.

"Stay there. Don't move yet," he insists, with his face in my hair. Tempting, but I push him away, and sit up despite the incredible dizziness that threatens to overtake me. The walls are bleeding; not bleeding but hemorrhaging long drooling lines of red. Here and there, bits of what appears to be tissue dot the otherwise smooth surface. Mark is leaning against the doorframe, wearing a crimson glove. His hand is entirely covered with the red muck and he doesn't seem to feel it nor the putrefying meaty weight of the creature's paw on his shoulder.

I stare at Eric, feeling my mouth open to ask him about it, then choke on the words. I can't breathe! A frozen hand is wrapped around my throat, and the rotting creature who had its hand on Mark's shoulder is before me, on his haunches. The stench makes me wretch; it fills my nose with the decomposing reek of one not dead long enough. It makes my head spin and I fall backwards against Eric, my fingers scrabbling at my neck for purchase on its hand so that I can breathe again and feel - nothing.

The light is dimming in the peripheral, and I suppose it's the fault of the black butterflies that keep fluttering at the edges of my vision. The want to steal me away into nothingness, even as I fight to stay conscious. The woman I envisioned when we arrived hovers over Eric's shoulder wearing a deadly sweet smile on her lips. The tip of her dagger is resting against the hollow of his ear and she is almost imperceptibly shaking her head. *Stay quiet or she will kill him now.*

I nod in return, and the putrid scent disappears as quickly as it had come, along with the hand at my throat. Fire couldn't burn more than my throat at that moment; if only it were hot.

Charley is at my side with her hand on Eric's shoulder and speaking in low tones in his ear. Her eyes are on Mark, who still stands where he was before, but his hand is now free of the bloody glove. As are the walls. "Let's get you up off the floor and to your room shall we," she says to me with a smile for Eric that does not reach her eyes, and not even a glance in my direction. There is an immediate seed of distrust that begins to grow in my chest. It causes physical pain, to distrust one of the few people that know me so well.

"Come on Moira, it's cold down here." Eric breaks the silence, pulling me up to my feet and standing behind me once he is sure I won't fall back.

This room is warm and feels safe. I don't want to leave here, and go where no one would hear me if I screamed for help. I can't bear to be alone right now. I feel his hands warm on my ribs, urging me to walk, and the pressure causes my heart to roar even though I had viciously muzzled it before leaving my bedchamber. Shivering, even through the sweater I wear, I shake him off, "Moira," he murmurs in distress, "please let me help you. I don't bite." He is touching me again, I give in and reach around to place my own arm around his waist and squeeze. "Liar," I half snarl, half laugh. Just this once. Terrified; I was terrified, if I was going to speak honestly to myself - the thought of being alone in this place and isolated is making me sick to my stomach.

Charley shakes her curls with a smirk and walks away, heading towards the wing where we all stay. What the hell is that show about?

Hoping to catch his eyes and ask silently, discover that they are already glued to mine. He shakes his head and shrugs. So he sees it too, and this gives me some measure of comfort. Around me, so much happens that almost everyone else misses. that at times I'm unsure if I am observing reality or a vision. Charley is still ahead but slowing her pace. She stops at my door, with her head down and appearing to stare at the ornate handle. It's difficult to tell with that curly hair falling forward. Unlike Charley, she is silent, with her hands clenched in fists at her side. "What the hell is she doing," Eric mutters, and I squeeze his hand. He calls her name and she doesn't respond.

Nothing; not twitch or a flutter to betray that she heard him. "You try," he urged and I cleared my throat lightly before raising my voice just a little bit.

"Hey Charley! Go ahead and open the door!" and she hitches a breath like someone poked her and relief floods my next words, "It's unlocked," I say in a louder voice, freezing as her head slowly lifts and turns towards me. Her face is a mask; completely expressionless and cold as though she had been carved from ice. If only that same emotionless gaze were in her eyes, but there is a malevolent glee dancing in them instead. Eric continues forward a step I catch up and point to Charley.

I am rooted in place by a fear that runs rampant in my veins, too afraid to take my eyes from her as the flight instinct battles with the logic in my mind. One insists that this *is not real* and the other shrieks **run!**

Eric steps towards her, taking his hand away and it is instantly cold. There is death here. I feel it in my bones like early frost on a summer windowpane. Eric hails her calmly as he removes the knife from his back pocket and flicks it open with open it with practiced ease.

Charley revolves mechanically, the smile that had been on her lips now widens into a toothy grin and her eyes narrow suspiciously on the small blade in Eric's hand. Nothing more than a whisper escapes my chest. It gets locked down from a roar and is immediately lost in the echoes of his footsteps.

She charges him and I break out of my frightened trance at last, and reach his side just as he throws his arm out. The blade of his knife catches her easily in the wafer thin hollow of her throat, but she just keeps coming. Charley's blood covers his hand and begins to patter rhythmically to the floor. She pushes further forward, her fingertips scrabbling at his face, and thankfully causing little damage to him and more to herself. She bit her nails habitually and I was never so grateful for this as I am now. I shove her backwards off the blade.

A sound that I hope never hear again assaults my ears; the wet slobber of the flaps of skin as she slides away from it and the boneless thud when she lands on the hard stone. Her head lands with a dull bonk, her hair flying up before landing and obscuring her face. I turn to look at Eric, horrified and heartbroken. He is staring at his hand with rapt attention, the knife's haft glistening with the last vestiges of life of our friend. I whisper his name, barely able to speak, and take a step closer to him when Charley's hand grasps my ankle, pulling me down beside with surprising strength.

A bloodcurdling howl that seems to seep from the walls reverberates from everywhere. Feeling sorry for the agony in that shriek, I realize its coming from me. My voice had finally unlocked. Charley rolls towards me with gnashing teeth snapping in the air. They make a dry clicking sound that reminds me of a ball point pen.

She means to bite so move it or lose it! I think to myself as I back away, narrowly missing a vicious snap of her teeth that would have surely severed whatever part of me she chose to close her jaws around. I can hear the running footsteps of the Calvary from down the hall. JP and Mark are leading the group at full speed towards where Charley has me cornered. She's got my back against the cold stone wall and is moving in for the kill. Her lips are moving in a rhythmic wave, speaking Latin as though she had been born to it and it makes no sense. The raised voices of the others do nothing to more to deter her, than my own pleading. She notices nothing except my desperate and terrified face with her cold and dead eyes and a falsely sweet smile still on her lips.

Jodee, steps forward and grabs Charley with both hands covering her ears and jerks hard up and to the left. A muffled report echoes in the now silent hallway.

Deafening and yet insignificant, as is her body hitting the stone floor again. I sit with my head on my knees and allow the tears to finally flow. From the gap between my arms I can see Charley's dead eyes staring at me accusingly with her hair spread across half of her face. "What the fuck happened here," Jodee demands, her voice trembling in anger as she crouches beside me. She tries to pull me into her embrace and I fight although I have no energy to try then lean against her.

"She went wrong, Jodee," Eric shouts, too loudly in the empty space, "she just went wrong Jodes and I had no choice. Moira saw something was off and I wouldn't listen to her. It's my fault." He wipes his hand on his jeans, leaving bloody streaks across the legs, effectively ruining them for further wear. I can't help but choke back the sour sting of vomit that climbs in my throat when he warily steps over Charley's body, to hold me to him.

VOICES BEHIND THE DOOR

AN EXCERPT FROM THE SELKIRK JOURNAL

Everyone has bedded down for the night, and most of us decided to bunk together for the sake of safety in a strange place. Also because I insisted that we all be close enough to hear if something happens. When something happens, because it will. It's an inevitability.

Whatever is here; that creature at the door, whomever that clearly demented woman is from my vision, they are insistent that this is their place and that we are unwanted here.
I tend to agree with them.

I was the odd man out on this trip and I drew the short match and so the prize: A room to myself. It's not something that I am upset about. After this afternoon, I need some solitude to recover and deal with the residual emotion.

I can't stop shaking and I couldn't sleep even if I tried. I did try but I keep hearing noises outside my door, even over the whine of that lame ass heater in the corner. The heater is loud, but that thing out there is louder. I suspect that it's Charley, or whatever malevolent spirit is wearing her like a costume. The thought makes me sick.

Mark called the owner this afternoon to inform him of Charley's death. The dismay in his voice was almost more than I could bear. It hurt to hear him suffering, mostly because he gave voice to what we were all feeling, and that frankly sucks.

But even more saddening was the incredulous expression on his face at our benefactor's curt response. He wouldn't tell us what was said; he just shook his fist and then walked away with his shoulders hunched and a sob in his throat. I think my first intuition about Mr. James was on the money.

JP and Eric lifted Charley's body onto a sheet from her room and look it away. There was nothing left of her but her blood on the floor as a reminder that we had participated in the murder of our friend. It's still there. The cleaning crew won't arrive for another six hours, according to the last telephone call JP received. Perhaps that's why she is still out there.

Mr. James, he of the Bentley arrived shortly after Mark's call, and wished to see where the events took place. I still find it odd that he wanted to see the pool of blood where our friend and colleague took her last breath.

Where we nearly lost our own lives. He stood there, for what seemed like forever with a smirk on his face before clapping his hands and telling us that he had hired people to come take care of the mess *and that the undertaker wagon would arrive in the morning as well to remove Charley from our care. That unbelievable son of a cockroach -*

How are we going to tell her family? What *will we tell her family?*

The door handle is rattling back and forth in its socket, half turns against the lock that I put on as we all took our leave to our rooms. More skittering movements from outside the door as well and I murmur that my invitation is revoked. Eric is sprawled in the bed behind me, barely covered in the blood-red sheets and with a smile on his face. I am glad for it. He stayed with me when I thought I would fall to pieces, and stayed when I did give in and cried until my chest hurt.

He kissed my tears away, gently holding my face in his, before giving release to the passion we both keep too deep in our hearts and away from prying eyes. Or so we think. We fell into each other's arms, tearing at our clothes and coming together in pleasure and grief until we lay spent. He fell to sleep with my head on his chest, wearing that same gentle and pleased smile that is on his lips now. We are both stupid, ignoring what has been building for too many years to mistake for lust or simple desire. I will tell him tomorrow, in the daylight, how I feel. For now, he has to sleep so he can be strong for what is coming. I also have to shoo him off to his room before the morning comes and the creatures stop stirring.

"Moira." The sinister surrusus outside my room door sends shivers up my spine. Jesus fuck that sound is giving me goosebumps, its so full of malice.

It's also a voice I know very well. I glance behind me again, hoping it hasn't awoken Eric from his much needed rest. Thankfully, he hasn't moved. For the time being, I am alone and Charley is outside my door, calling my name and clumsily trying to turn the knob.

I want to go home.

HIDDEN DANGERS

The clock says 2:13 am and someone is screaming out in the hallway. It feels like I just got to sleep and I probably just did. I came back to bed and lay awake until the moon faded from the window and then finally, I cuddled up to Eric and fell asleep to the sound of his heartbeat. Now this.

Eric jolts up out of a dead sleep, breathing fast with wide eyes. Still dressed, I bolt from the bed and throw open the door. The hall is deserted but the racket seems to be coming from JP and Jake's room. With a deep breath, I run into the deserted hall, thankful to see nothing that might threaten to stop me.

My bare feet slide in the now cold pool of blood and I nearly tumble to the floor. Speed is my friend as I regain my balance and fly towards the source of the scream, leaving bloody footprints on the cold stone floor. There are other prints as well, some dragging and smeared as though some dead thing walked through the puddle. *Ghosts don't leave prints*, I tell myself as I burst into the room and the horror of poor JP at the fireplace mouth, trapped. Jake is manic, pacing with his hands in his hair one moment and fumbling at the mantle the next. This makes little sense.
Why is JP stuck in the fireplace?

"What the blue *fuck* is going on!" Eric barks, brushing past me to reach JP first. I approach the men warily after observing JP's lips turning blue and seeing him beginning to sag. His arm is stuck in the wall; why this is happening I can't even begin to imagine – I know the how, but why he would go against the rules boggles me.

JP's elbow is swollen and turning an unhealthy shade of puce. A few inches below that, the bones of his lower arm are poking through the skin like jagged teeth. Beside me, Eric pukes into the ash basket that is sitting on the hearth.

"How the hell did this happen?" I ask Jake, covering JP with the blanket that he had retrieved from the bed. He opens his mouth to tell me but it's JP that answers me, with hazy eyes barely focusing and a drunk man's slur, "The wall opened, Moira! Like those old movies we watch? Jake and me were just going to sleep and the wall *opened*. Like magic!!" JP's eyes were alive, sparkling with life and I felt that familiar ache in my chest. "Charley was in there. I tried to save her Moira. I tried but when I reached for her, the wall slammed shut. She's trapped in there. I can feel her touching my hand."

After last night, I can believe almost anything. Charley, or whatever spirit is possessing her body, is the same one that greeted me and invited me, invited us, in. I accepted and now they are paying for it. "It's alright, Johnny you tried. Charley is fine and you will be too." It's a lie, a blatant one, but one I hoped would become a truth.

Scanning the room, my gaze stops on Eric, knowing full well that we were in trouble if we couldn't get JP free. He nods at me and does his own visual sweep. He agrees that there is nothing close enough at had to do anything useful with in here. I had to go find tools. "JP? Johnny honey, I need to go find you help. Eric and Jake are going to stay with you and try to find a way to open the wall again. Can you be strong? It won't be long and I'll be back. I promise." He nods vacantly, as a flood of profanity rings in the hall. The rest of the team were at last awake.

Perfect timing. I'd need some help to find the tool I needed to free him. "Okay JP. I'm going now." I know he will last as long as he can, but he certainly can't survive this way for very long. Jodee skids to a stop with a horrified gasp and I spin her around and drag her towards the door. Jodee is demanding more information, and protesting her enlistment, but I tell her to hush, then yell out instructions. "If he drops, he will probably die so help him!"

"He might die anyway," Eric mutters and given what I had in mind to free him, I agree, although I refuse to give voice to that, not while JP can still hear. Those words cannot be his death knell.

In the hall, I fill in my unwilling volunteer as quickly as I can and without breaking stride. "Jodee. Go to the kitchen. We need boiling water, a lot of it.

They have some kind of machine in there that I used at breakfast. Towels. A belt if you can. I don't know if any one is wearing one but safer than sorry. Hurry Jodes, okay? We don't have time for dawdling. If you love JP ..." She stares stunned for a moment then dashes off in the direction of the massive kitchen without asking any further questions. What exactly would I say to her? *"He's going to die so this is probably useless, but hurry anyway?"*

There is a library through the door to my left and unthinkingly, but focused on my friend suffering back in his room, I spy a frame on the wall. People frame the strangest things. It is heavy but I rip it from the wall and hurl it to the ground with every ounce of strength in me, and shield my face. The glass sprays everywhere, bouncing and glinting in the sunlight. Functionality in beauty; the tool I so desperately need skitters across the carpet.

I grab it by the blade on the run and feel its still sharp teeth biting into my palm. I'm sure I'll need stitches and a tetanus shot later.

A loud clattery sound of metal on gravel announces Jodee's arrival and just in time. She has found a small rolling table to transport a huge pot of steaming water and piles of towels on the shelf below. "It's going to be bloody. If you have a weak stomach, take Eric in the hall. We don't need hysterics, okay?" Jodee nods and begins pushing the table as fast as safely possible. To her credit she doesn't spill a drop. My hand is dripping onto the floor and I shake the excess off to rid myself of the slimy feel. Mr. James probably won't be impressed with the mess but he isn't the concern here. JP is.

The room is full of people; the living and dead and all eyes were watching JP with dismay. Someone had gotten him one of the chairs from the sitting room and he is kneeling and sagging against Mark.

"What are hell are you going to do with that?" Mark demands, his face white with sick suspicion. Shaking my head, I don't offer an answer. For no other reason than not thinking more than one step ahead than necessary in order to keep my sanity. Jake is wearing a belt, and I need it.

"Jake! Take off your belt and wrap it as tightly as you can around his bicep. *Tight as you can*, got it?" He gapes, aghast and doesn't react. *"We don't have time for this!"* I shake my head, and grab for his middle, undoing the belt and pulling it back against the pins that hold it in place. He jumps slightly, pushing my hands away as he removes the leather strap and does as I ask. JP moans as the belt tightens enough to push the sides of his skin out from under it. "JP? Can you hear me? This is going to hurt. You *must stay still* no matter how hard it is. Don't fight Moira. Do you hear?" Jake shouts into the face of the gravely injured man.

He nods slightly, straightening his spine under his own power and through gritted teeth. The old bone saw seems to gain weight as I place the blade against the palest part of his arm, and drag it back with every ounce of power I possess. His flesh splits and spurts blood all over my face and hands. the bones that had been crushed by the weight of the stone door withdrew back into the skin with the loss of pressure.

Behind me I hear the harsh grinding sounds of several people puking their hearts onto the floor, and in once case, the thump of a body hitting the floor. All of it is white noise and meaningless in the face of the task at hand. Jake grunts, then pulls the belt tighter, while I continue sawing the damaged limb free of JP's body. Jodee whispers Logan's name sickly behind me as. Eric staggers under the extra weight when JP finally passes out. It's a relief that I welcome both for JP and me.

Now, the muscles relax, making it easier to finish the last of this unreal chore. With one last massive pull, JP's body falls free of his trap, and lands unmoving. onto the hearth. "We need to cauterize it," Jodee sobs, her voice ill and faint. She hands me a small blowtorch that she must have found in the kitchen as she prepared the water. "A little trickier than Crème brûlée but in a pinch."

I have no clue how to start the blowtorch and hand it back to her, then yank the belt tight again "Where the hell is Jake? Can someone help me here?" Jake has disappeared leaving me to manage on my own. There is a hiss and a popping sound nearby and Mark hands me the torch, while Jodee soaks a towel in the hot water and wipes down the wound so that I can stop the bleeding. "Deep breath Moira, hold it to the wound, not long. The wound will burn fast, so just until it is sealed. Do you want me to do it?"

Eric's hands are on my shoulder and I shake them off. JP howls in his unconscious hell while I burn the end of his raw and ruined stump. It sizzles under the flame, the skin on the edges bubbling in the heat and for some odd reason reminds me of fondue beef.

Logan is sitting on the floor by the window, with an I-told-you-so expression that inflates the guilt I am already suffering. We need to find some way to out of here before we end up like the last team.

Death and Elinor's Madness

AN EXCERPT FROM THE SELKIRK JOURNAL

JP died. He bled out about twenty minutes after I amputated his arm. He was cold and we covered him up and started a fire but it wasn't enough. I tried but it wasn't enough. He needed a skilled surgeon not some clearly untrained hack. I tried, but I failed. How am I going to live with the fact that I killed my friend? How many more have to die before we get out of this forsaken place?

What am I going to say to his parents?

Eric called the families of Charley and JP. I couldn't. Just watching the devastated expression break when he tried to explain to them was so hard to watch. It broke my heart when I was sure it had been torn out already. He also called Mr. James, who made the arrangements for a funeral home and cleaners to come immediately but never showed himself. When the undertakers came, I wasn't' around. I understand they took JP and Charley both. I'm glad that she is gone. It sounds cruel but there it is. Whatever is here, was using her to trap us.

There are six of us left now, all of us are watching each one another carefully for signs of whatever madness controls the atmosphere of Selkirk Keep. The lawns and gardens are manicured and the furnishings so well cared for that they seem new. I hate it here.

The beauty is deceiving; while it seems perfect on its face, under the mask it is nothing more than a cadaverous, invidious monster, bent on destroying us all.

The doctor that came with the funeral home van stitched my palm and bandaged it, then gave me a tetanus shot. She sewed me up while chatting in a low calm tone that inevitably kept me calm too. I know it was an effort to ease the shaking and I appreciated it. But all while, her anxiousness was palpable. Her swift but obvious eye flickers to the bookshelf and the doorway spoke volumes and I knew she could sense the malevolent sprit that had been quietly observing us a from atop the bookshelf. Whether or not she can see whatever lingers here, is still anyone's guess but the way she nearly ran out the door when he was through was enough. No words were needed. I only wish I could have gone with her.

Eric and I are now sharing my room. Mark, Jodee and Jake and Logan, are sharing the adjoining suite. Closer quarters means safer nights. The cleaners have been and gone, having left no traces of the blood that poured out of our friends behind. I'm glad for that. What I'm not glad for is the way that our group is being whittled down one by one, or the way we have taken to peering into rooms or around corners before entering. **Or** *the fact that there is that creature that shows it self every time someone's death is imminent. It has taken to following us everywhere, wearing it's mansuit.*

He's here now, standing by the door that leads to the other suite, staring holes in the back of my head and watching Eric as he shuts down some of the equipment. With so few of us left, we can't possibly cover the entire place and our cameras are having technical issues constantly so we can't leave them to record either.

I suspect that the woman in my vision, in my reality, is responsible. She is the one holding us hostage here. The other is her lackey. I have proof of it now, although I'm not sure exactly how it will help or even improve our situation. Perhaps it is serendipity or fate, but I found it while I was cleaning up the glass from the frame that held the hacksaw in the library.

Mr. James is very upset, and raved at Eric for over an hour about how he trusted us to treat his residence with respect and on and so forth. The fact that his residence was trying, and succeeding, to kill us off one by one seems of no consequence to him. I've begun to despise everything about him really. He's got an air of superiority, something akin to an entitlement issue that goes along with the title I suppose. He expects to be given whatever he demands.

Back to the book. It was sitting with its pages facing out on a bottom shelf that obviously hadn't been touched in forever. I might have missed it myself if I hadn't been on my hands and knees picking up the tiny pieces of glass that were resisting all other methods. There was one small sliver of glass that landed in front of that oddly placed book, and the shelf was covered in dust bunnies thick enough to eat a human hand. I agreed to picking up my mess, not to clean up someone else's and left a line in the grit without a thought to anything more.

I pulled it from the shelf, and set it on the table to wipe my fingers on my jeans. It feels wrong and distasteful; old but somehow still new and alive. It is an odd history that reads like more like a diary, and it may be at that. The pages are thick and pliable, and filled edge to edge with a plainly feminine script.

It didn't seem of consequence the first time I left the room, or the second. But this time I felt moved to take a break and take a read. Truly, I wasn't very interested in it but it called me and so it seemed to make sense to at least see what the story is about. So many local historians of the time, and they simply wrote their impressions; why should book be any different? On first scan, it doesn't seem to be different, but it is. Written as a diary, this appears to be a true account of feudal King Calum, who we knew was murdered. What we didn't know, should this be true, was that he was murdered by his wife.

Her first act of betrayal was to kill the houseman, her husband's personal valet. There is no name mentioned, although there is a drawing of this unfortunate soul. This book says that she mutilated him, this houseman, chopped off his fingers to the second knuckle, his nose and his penis as well and left him spread-eagled on the King's bed.

She then entered the hall where King Culen was addressing and feeding his soldiers, something she was forbidden to do, and stuffed the dismembered parts of the houseman into the mouth of her husband. She cut his throat in front of a room full of soldiers and claimed the crown for herself. A balsey move for a woman of that era, and lucky for her that she wasn't killed on the spot. Queen Elinor, his new bride of less than a year, was also purported to be not only mad, but a witch. Of that accusation there is no further information, only that one small tidbit.

An internet search yielded much more morbidly interesting information, that though I can't substantiate, has begun to grow a pattern in my mind that I can't seem to let go of. Through the centuries, there have been seven murders. Every seven years. six people in a household, connected or not, are all discovered dead.

The numbers don't seem to add up to anything, although there is always a survivor it appears. I'll have to search further.

The deaths of those innocent people are terrible deaths too. No other team had been invited since the last, but one account, that wasn't Logan, spoke of their investigation and the footage they collected was disturbing. For the first time since I saw the name Selkirk Keep, I am truly scared for the first time in my life.

One other thing that I need to make note of before I go back to work. One person in each of these accounts was proven to have blood ties to Selkirk Keep, in some way or form. I know that I don't have a blood tie to this place, or I'm sure that my parents would have told that story, and I'm sure that Eric doesn't either. He would have brought it up before now, wouldn't he?

HISTORY'S HOLLOW GAME

"Hey Moira? Could you come in here a second?" Eric's voice startles me from my account notes throough the mic I'm wearing. I'd forgotten it was there, to be truthful and now my train of thought has been derailed enough to make me get up and slam my diary shut. There is a tone of suppressed excitement in his voice that makes me smile. He must have found something on the recordings. "Yes, Eric, give me a couple. Travel time and all that." He snickers lightly in response. With the box under one arm and my diary in the other hand, I can't help but think to myself, *At least we will have something to show for the hell and loss,*

I think as I enter the hall and see him leaning close to one of the monitors. Jodee, Mark and Logan are with him, all bent over and watching the screen in delight and dismay. "What have you found?" I ask by way of announcing my presence, and drop the box of glass bits on the nearest table. They all shush me Peering over Eric's shoulder, I see an impossibility on the monitor. The first glance makes my heart beat faster, the second steals my breath. We finally had concrete proof that we aren't alone.

The figure on the screen moves slowly from one end to the other, pausing in the middle of the room twice. Once it just stood and unmoving for a few seconds, and the second to stare at the desk where I often sit at while writing my impressions in my diary. That's where it is now, with its hand on the smooth black top of my laptop.

I elbow Eric hard in the ribs, irritated that I was not made aware of a camera in my room and concerned the others may have seen more than they should have.

He winces then smiles at me, licking his lips lasciviously before pointing back to the screen. Shaking my head, I return my attention to the monitor and feel my blood freeze instantly as the figure looks deliberately at the camera. Whomever is in my room is wearing my face. "Is this live?" I choke out, feeling a chill travel up and down my body as the creature on the screen stares back at us.

"Yes," Jodee replies absently, moving slightly away from me yet never taking her eyes off of what was playing out before us, "It's happening now. Whatever that is, it's in your room and has been looking through your belongings. You are you, right?" This pisses me off and I make for my room, grabbing an earpiece from the nearby table and tossed it to Jake.

"Turn it on, keep it on. I want to know what the hell I'm walking into." I stalk from the room and down the hall towards the imposter that resembles me and to beat its purpose out of it with bare-fisted if I have to. A chorus of dismay sounds behind me but I don't stop. I can't stop even if I wanted to. Something has my free will in its fist and has me prisoner. Eric trots up in front of me and holds his hands out, begging me to stop. He tries to hold me back holding onto my upper arms, but he just slides backwards. "Moira stop! Please think! You can't go down there alone. Let us come with you at least. All of us together, all of the time right, until this is finished? Isn't that what you said?" He reminds me of my own words.

I will say no more. The mics are on and we are being listened to; be damned if I will provide a free show when he won't even admit that we are a couple. "Come if you are coming, stay if you're not."

I move around him and continue down the hall with a deep seed of trepidation growing in my chest. I continue in silence, determined to know what in Hades Secret Birdcage is going on here and knowing that no matter how hard he tries, he can't stop it from happening. Eric is hot on my heels, and bangs into me as I stop short at the end of the hall that leads to our room and whatever lurks there. "Moira, what the hell ..." he stops short, his voice barely a whisper in my ear. His arms are warm against my ribs, and I'm sure he can feel the fearthump of my heart against them. "The blood is back," I moan, pointing down the hall, to the pool of blood next to the door.

It was back, and so was the Lady's lackey, nearly hidden in the late day shadows. The dark and sinister smile on his rotted lips is almost pleasant in its evil regard. A sharp intake of breath tells me Eric sees it too, the impossible red seeping into the cracks of the ancient stone floor.

The creature is staring at us, its brows furrowed in suspicion as Eric leans closer to my ear and his arms tighten around me out of his own fear. "Does that mean she is back too? And JP? What else is there Moira? What do you see?"

"The same creature that greeted me when we arrived," I respond in normal tones. I refuse to whisper and hide, and I will not give in to the terrormongering that threatens our every waking moment. I pry myself free, admonishing Eric to stay put and hoping against hope that he would actually listen this time. Fed-up with the games, I march directly to the lackey and glare directly into his insipid grin. The fragrance of his decomposition is so strong in my nose that it is making my stomach lurch, "What do you want? Why are you here? *Why are you doing this?*" I demand, the anger I'd been feeling all day finally bubbles up and out.

"Because of you. You are here, finally. Daughter of my womb, the one we have waited for," intones a woman a behind me. The Lady who beckoned me, the one who threatened Eric, and murdered my friends. The one who brought them back again.

I can hear Eric speaking to someone, but am unable to look away from the creature wavering in front of me. Improbable beauty, she must have been handsome in life, but now she resembles little more than a leprous hard rode monster. "Stop. You don't need them." I'll stay if you let them go. You've waited for me? You have me, willingly." The hallway rings with her laughter, rough and full of contempt through vocal cords that sound like they have been treated with a grater. I can hear Jake's voice, too, in my ears. Eric screaming my name, warning me of what has appeared behind me. I can barely understand him in his terror.

Perhaps he has seen her with his own eyes, or the sound of her glee has reached him. A single word sounds a bell of horrific knowledge in my heart. Charley. I break contact with Lackey and turn with a smile to face the next test. It wears Charley's shell like a glove.

No matter what else transpires, this thing is not my friend, nor is it human. "Charley, or whatever you are. What the hell were you doing in my room?" I ask rudely, feigning nonchalance over the silver tingle of fear that runs up my spine.

She smiles, and the chills end. She is not malignant; her soul has not been tarnished by the evil of this place. She has simply not gone home, and has instead, for some unfathomable reasons chosen to stay and deliver her message rather than going to Source. She shakes her head and whips her eyes to Eric, and with wary confidence, holds out her hand to me. Unafraid for the first time in days, I take it willingly.

Her grip is solid smoke, as cold as a prairie winter's night, and still it holds mine with the same warmth it had before. I can hear her speaking to me, her tone imploring and that is as usual as it comes. Charley tries to take Eric's hand; the sensation of chill that touches him surprises and he jerks away from me, from what he once dreamed of experiencing. The whole situation is heartbreaking to observe. "Put your hand back honey. Remember when you wanted proof? It's Charley, Rico. Just Charley," I murmur to him, using her nickname for him and touching his cheek with my other hand. His sleep deprived face wears his weary fear like a mask.

"It's alright, Eric. This is important to me, to her too; please, put your hand back down. She won't hurt you," I promise him quietly. Eric backs away from me slowly, holding his hands up in defence, and shakes his head then turns and bolts back down the way we came.

I'm confused and turn to look at Charley, who hangs her head in defeat. There was no way in 80's horror hell that he was going to get away running away when he lectures me constantly on doing just that. I was going to get to the bottom of this, and I wanted answers *now*. Charley's hand returns to nothing and I frankly forget she is there on my mission to hunt down the coward that I love.

When I arrive, The Great Hall is completely devoid of even the normal ambient noises that exist everywhere. The eerie quiet makes my ears buzz and I slow around the corner with my nerve endings on fire. Jake runs into me at full tilt and knocks me down. He was watching over his shoulder instead of where he was going and now stands above me with his hand over his mouth, making a wet urking sound behind it. "Moira, Jebus Krispies, your eyes, what happened to your *eyes*?"

Jake asks me with horror in his voice while he lifts me from the floor, and sets me on my feet again before taking my arm, and gently leading me to where the rest sit stunned. I don't understand; I can see as I always did, although my surroundings do seem a little more real, more there.

Jake pushes me into a chair opposite Eric, the one that faces the windows and the gardens beyond. My anger at him hasn't had time to dissipate, not yet and Eric knows it. Mark crouches in front of me, his elbows resting on my knees as he regards at me with an expression that I am coming to despise. *"You left me,"* I snarl at Eric, bulldozing past Mark to the window, and wrap my arms around myself. I'm coming apart at the seams; nothing seems right - the man that I gave myself to has abandoned me, and sits there like a damned stone statue in the chair.

Jodee is at my side, instead of him, with her chin on my shoulder and her arms around my waist. She is trying not to comfort and somehow doing it all the same, thankfully. "Come sit back down. You don't understand what's happening and you need to. Please, just come and listen okay?"

Letting my eye roam over the landscape gives me a moment to hold back tears and regain control over my raging emotions. It's another fight lost, as they over run my lids and scorch trails down my cheeks. "Moira, come on, don't cry. It'll be okay, I promise, just come, open your mind and listen to us for a change," Jodee coaxes I nod at her, finding it odd that my face is dry when it should be wet from my tears, then spin around to face what remains of our team. Jodee takes my arm gently, and I allow her to lead me forward, too tired to fight. My eyes feel tired and sore. I'm sure its from the crying, and this doesn't add to my otherwise frustrated disposition.

Taking my chair once more, I look down at my hands, observing how they writhe in my lap and pull them apart, choosing to tuck them under my thighs to stop their incessant twisting.

They always did give my anxiety away. Eric leans forward, speaking softly and places his too warm hand on my knee, as he does when he is hurting and afraid. I don't understand what he has to be afraid of, and say as much, then watch him flinch and jerk his hand away with an ashamed wince. "Honey, can you see?" he asks with a rasp in his voice. Why is he crying?

"What kind of question is that? Of course I can see! I see you crying, and Jake looking out into the entry, Jodee is leaning over Mark's chair, whispering in his ear and making him smile. *Yes, I can see.* Why?" I snap at everyone in the room, hearing the thin tone in my voice and hating the way it sounds. I'm exasperated, and it colours every word.

The panic rat has begun to gnaw at my insides, not just running amok but truly biting. Logan returns from wherever he had disappeared to, holding a small frame in his hands.

There is a small fluttering moth I call tension twirling where my heart used to be; Logan is making me nervous - he is too pale, with distaste on his lips and a stiffening of his spine. He stands in front of me, with that frame he had with him before me so that I can see my reflection. Nothing in this place is real and that image in the glass is just the same. Still, all of my senses keep screaming at me to run far and as fast as I can, but all that I can do is sit and shake my head, and hope to make some sense of what I am seeing. It's impossible - my reflection is a lie, another glamour set up by the demons that reside here to trick my mind –there is no way that what that imposter in the mirror is showing could be true.

"Moira? Do you understand why I panicked? I was scared and I reacted badly. It's no excuse but -" Eric says quietly, regretful. His voice breaks, and shatters a little bit of my heart with it, "Please forgive me. It was visceral."

It was the next eight words that hit home harder than anything else he could have said. "Charley took your eyes, and I was afraid." How could I have been so blind? She stole my eyes from my face even as I watched her. I felt bad for her! And now – but *how*? - Replaying the incident in my mind, I pull my hands from under my thighs and watch as my reflection raises them to my cheeks. The fingers are cold as ice and in spite of it, there is only agony when the tips touch my eyes; my skin is nothing more than flaming nerve endings.

"I was bleeding and didn't know?" I realise then that she wasn't hanging her head in defeat.

No, she was laughing, and looking down so that I wouldn't see. Why am I not reading right? I should have seen through it. "I can still see. She took my eyes but I can still see everything. How is this possible?" I can't leave this place; I've tried but they thwart me at every turn. It doesn't mean that I can't find my way outside, blinded or not.

I need to think and clear my mind, and its rapidly becoming a desperate situation. "I need air. **Don't follow me**," I tell them, hearing the scream close and choking it back down before I could speak the words I needed to. What else could they do to me now, these spirits, after this? Kill me? I stand, hearing my friends' denials and refusals to let me go alone. Eyeballing each one, I stare long and hard, taking in the frightened expressions with little emotion, "*Do Not Follow Me.*"

I repeat, striding from the room, not looking back nor having any desire to do so.

They are forgotten as my thoughts turn to the time ahead. These people need to know what exactly we are up against. No more games.

MIRACLE EYES

There are benevolent spirits here, as well as the malevolent. I've seen and felt them since our arrival; even spied them in corners and on the stairs, simply observing our movements with outright curiosity in at least one case. Thankfully, it is benign interest and I welcome it. They are here now, these gentle souls; they line the wide hallway that I wander aimlessly down, and I am finally at ease for the first time since we came here.

I suspect that Mr. James is the familiar of the evil ones; the slave who brings fresh meat for these monsters to feed upon, seven each year. Somebody here must hold a blood tie but who?

`Someone; how else would he be able to bring a blood relative here time after time? I will need to do some research before I can move any further. If I have the time to do so. They seem to be playing games with the electronic devices and hiding my pens.

The winding staircase to the roof is on my right, and I turn into the doorway to gaze in awe at the brightness that illumines it. Each step is filled with Light and Love, those spirits of the lost that remain here, trapped, instead of taking the journey Home. A translucent youth, a young man dressed in the finery that the mist graces him with touches my arm as I pass, his light fills me with peace and concern. I stop and look into his eyes, and feel the pain creep back into my awareness. His smile is sweet and kind, shining with the love of the saved. It makes me want to cry, but my injuries will no longer permit it.

A harsh sob tears my throat as I sink to the floor, the realization of what I've endured rushes in and steals all my strength. The young man whispers gently, his touch is both cold and warm, and it explains everything as easily as 42* and twice as vague. What I come away with is that I can stop everything if I am strong enough to sacrifice myself. The knowledge brings me no relief. In no way does it make the situation better, except that I now know that if I take myself out of the equation, things change.

Some of the people I care about are still sitting in the Great Hall discussing their own options, and the next actions will decide whether or not the others will walk out of here alive. I'm strong enough for that. He kisses my forehead as though he is a father bestowing love upon a cherished child; with his hands on either side of my face, that kiss was the gentlest and kindest gesture I've experienced in my life.

His lips leave a chilled impression on my flesh and the strength I doubted I had was renewed with it. I had enough of it to stagger to my feet, and continue climbing. I can smell the fresh outdoors through the narrow slits in the walls. The Wispy Ones tell me that once the castle defenders used to fire arrows at invading armies through them. That now, they were little more than decorations that allowed the real world in and that fewer and fewer believe that history is as deadly as their reality.

Each step is a chore, the weight of awareness should be heavy and yet I feel liberated. The elephant that had settled on my shoulders after the first vision lifted with the first rays of sunlight on my face. It's so bright that, if I believed in such a place, I am sure that this is what Heaven feels like. So much light after the darkness of the residual death in the walls of Selkirk Keep that it steals my breath away. Had the Gods and Goddesses above approved of my choice?

Only They know for sure, but it comes down to the one thing They cannot possibly control. Free will. It is my choice, and I alone will pay whatever eternal penalty that came with it, should there be such a levy on the lives of my friends. I couldn't save Charley or JP. Perhaps this would pay for all.

The countryside is vast and beautiful from this height. It was how I always had imagined the colour emerald, we were surrounded by delicious scenery and the occasional spotting of heavily perfumed gardens filled the air with sweetness. Small homes that once belonged to the feudal king that ruled over this land, and now to the more well-to-do of the modern world, dot the landscape. They are all well-kept and idyllic, much like the gardens that surround this fallacy of beauty. I climb on top of the thick stone barrier that holds me back from plummeting to the earth, for now.

The breeze in my hair, playfully tossing it here and there was like coming home; it welcomed me with its strong fingers that rustled at my clothing. Just below the thick and fluffy cotton balls clouds, against the blue sky seabirds fly - *they really do look like m's, like Eric's eyes.* The sprits are everywhere, surrounding me and their voices numb the fear that is threatening to overwhelm. I know it is the right choice. The numbness is a blessing, and when it steals my sight, and my world is at last dark, the sensation of hands on my back that softly urge my forward are nothing less than comforting. The only regret is that my friends will find my broken and lifeless body and that they will never understand why. Perhaps that's a bigger blessing.

"What the *fuck* are you doing?!" a voice screams from behind me, startling me from the welcome tumble into darkness that promised to envelope me and causing me to stumble, disoriented.

I feel the stone fall away from beneath my feet, and pinwheel my arms to regain my balance. *I'm not ready!* Rough hands grab the back of my slacks and yank me backwards onto the hard floor. My head hurts, my eye sockets throb as my head hits the rock, once, and bouncing back to hit again. Stars sparkle on the black butterfly wings in my inner vision as my stomach lurches in anger.

"Why Moira *why*? Why would you do this to me?" Eric. Damn him, I was so close to releasing him from his invisible prison and he *ruined* it. My vision comes back in a roaring stream, an overload to my aching mind, and I see him; raging eyes as blue as the summer sky demanding an answer for my betrayal with tears threatening to spill. I can't afford to relent so I shove away, refusing his help to stand and using the edge of the wall to pull myself up from the ground.

It's a fight not to glare in his direction, or to wrap my hands around his throat and throttle him til he collapses. It wars with the need to wrap my arms around him and stay there forever. He takes the choice from my hands, and enfolds me in his embrace and sobs into my hair. His tears hot and full of hurt. "I told you not to follow me. Don't you ever listen to me?" I mutter into his chest, my hands in fists on his back, thumping once, twice to make my point before leaning back to wipe his face.

Eric shakes his head, admonishing me for even considering taking my own life and I thought I comprehend his anger, he doesn't understand my reasons; I can't explain it to him, not now and probably not ever. The Lady of the House is back; that evil bitch is determined to destroy every life she touches, and now she stands behind the man I love with her teeth bared and her long, sharp nails poised at the side of Eric's head.

I have little doubt that she would drive it through bone and into his brain should I go against her wishes. In response to my inner dialogue, the bitch gives me a smirk that would enrage me if it didn't come with a vision that I could have done without.

Logan reaches for the sharp pencil that lies on the spiral notebook where he has been making notes. He rubs at his face in a tied gesture while going over the footage that the remaining cameras have caught. The words on the paper make no sense, the gibberish and non-consequential thoughts fill the page but keep a cadence nonetheless. The Lackey stands behind him with his rotting hands on his shoulders and whispers into his ear. Logan raises the razor point to his right eye. Without hesitation, he rams it into the fluid filled orb, and straight through until only the eraser is visible. Blood splatters the monitor screen as he falls backwards, and jitters on the floor - thick red fluid gushes from his ear.

My body stiffens against Eric in unconscious response to what I had just experienced. There is no air, even though my breath tears in and out of my lungs and wonder if this is how I will die. "You need to go and check on Logan. I'm fine, just *go!*" It's as though he hasn't heard me, and without asking for any more information, Eric leads me back to the door, and down the stairs, refusing to utter even a word to me in his anger. The faces of the hopeful dead are now fallen in sorrow, looking away as I descend. I know that I've failed them and my friends; the knowledge nearly breaks me but there is no way to change what's happened. There will be other opportunities.

The Lackey lurks at the bottom of the stairway, attempting to block our way with small, hateful smile upon his rotted lips. In that moment, I was lost in my hatred and spat at the echo of a sad little man.

"You've won, now get the hell out of our way," I snarl at him, feeling Eric pull me closer. Whether it is to protect me or hold me back, I'm unsure. Lackey steps away, his maggot ridden fingers reach out to stroke my hair as we pass; with the slightest touch, the visions of things to come inundate my mind along with a bone shuddering grinding sound fills the hall followed by a screech of pain. And as always the precursor of death, the Lackey laughs at the agony of the living.

"Go!" I'll make it there - *go save Logan*, if you can." He nods and runs at full speed back towards the Great Hall. The screaming has faded, now only the sounds of my own breath and footsteps are left, although other presences loiter nearby. The voices are raised again, the panic is evident and it is yet another dagger in the chest Logan's body is exactly has it had been in my vision, laying prone and lifeless.

The blood pooled around his head is almost too red to be real, but not as surreal as the unbelievably pink eraser deep in the socket of his eye. Jodee sits against the far wall, under the same window that I stood staring out of not so long ago and gnaws on her knuckles with tears streaming down her wan face. Mark is crouched beside her, speaking softly and glancing out of the window at the sky, where the seabirds fly. Jake is there too, firmly holding onto my arm and trying leading me away from the carnage. He succeeds, but not before my foot lands on the edge of the pool.

Now the floor has bloody footprints like some ridiculous crime comic. All I can do is sob and wonder how I am supposed to end the death when every attempt to do so is thwarted at every step. He looks up at me with misty eyes, and shakes his head.

"It was fine! There was nothing odd at all. I mean, we were watching you - we forgot to take down that rooftop cam, sorry When Eric saw you come through that door, he took off and told us to stay here and stay together. After you climbed up on the ledge - Moira, what were you thinking? -, Logan went really quiet. He jus sat there watching then grabbed the pencil and...and, ah God."

The sound of Mark's devastation echoes my own, and his tears are the only ones I can cry. Embracing his shoulders, he sinks his forehead onto my neck to mourn as I can no longer do. We've all lost so much in such a short period of time. His words are muffled but clear enough to make me sigh. "It's her doing this You were going to jump, weren't you?" he asks me, lifting his head and wiping his face with the back of his hand. I refuse to lie and simply return his open request with empty eyes and nod. "She's here, standing behind you. She's always around you. I know what you were thinking now and thank you for trying. I'm next, aren't I?"

"Yes, and it won't be nice. She will make sure of it. I'm sorry, Mark. So fucking sorry," I murmur, feeling my eye sockets begin to burn and ache, filling with tears that can never be shed.

A BOOK OF THE DEAD

AN EXCERPT FROM THE SELKIRK JOURNAL

It reads like a book of the dead. Charley, JP Logan, Mark. Poor Mark is gone. He suffered, but thankfully not for too long. His screams were so horrible that I wanted to bash his head in for a heartbeat so as not to prolong his pain and ours. Eric shot me a warning glare and I withdrew back into my own head, where I could scream along with Mark. I can't feel anymore. I can't See, spiritually since Mark died.

Somehow, I'm blocked out of my senses for the first time in my recollected memory, and its all been done by the daemons that live here.

This morning I heard a terrific racket outside the bedroom window, and it sounded like the world was exploding around us. There were so many shouting voices. The window provided me nothing more than a dusky impression of fighting men, and the flashes of their swords clanging as they warred. Plenty of unfriendly male banter, threats and it was all absolutely there/not there. I'm honestly not sure what's real anymore.

Eric was standing behind me, his sleep warm body close and comforting. "It's not real. It can't be real. It's the middle of the night, and there is no one here but us." He kissed the nape of my neck softly then whispered in my ear,

"They are fighting in the daylight and its far too early to be concerned about things we cannot change. Come back to bed, love. You need your sleep." He was right. I did need my sleep. I was exhausted, and still am.

When I turned to kiss him, terrible words filled my head.

Aye Milady, I shall set the boys to digging. A wooden crate as before?

I heard it; the smoky malevolence of that voice still sends a silver chill down my spine. I know what they have planned and I have my own wrench to throw into the works. A benefit to being blocked is that they can't read my thoughts. Nodding, I follow him back to bed, and said nothing until we had settled under the covers alone. Stroking his cheek, that seeming never empty pool of desire that I'd kept hidden so long burbled to the surface. I finally said the words I'd been holding on to for too long. "I love you, Eric. All this time we've wasted denying how I felt, when we could have had so much more. Can you forgive me?" He smiled at me, his hand brushing ng my hair from my cheek, and answers with his lips.

In his arms, I found the strength to go forward, knowing full well the pain I was about to inflict on him would leave him little solace. When our love was spent, we lay together and talked until his breath came deep and even.

I'll leave a note, to explain and hope that when they see the footage, in the daylight hours, they will understand. I know that Eric won't understand, and why would he?
I'd rather they survive, than to have to suffer through the rest of the losses that are inevitable. I pray to the Above that they will all forgive me.

MY LEGACY

When I could move and not worry about waking him, I dash off a letter by hand and leave a sticky note with my laptop password on the lid of my closed device. It will have to do I kiss him goodbye, and hear him whisper my name as he rolls over. I don't want to go but I'm desperate to escape this Hell I've been put in. With my decision made, I cross quickly to the door, and ease it open to peer out into the hallway. Scanning out of habit with my mind's eye for any movement, though its sight had been taken from me.

I hear nothing more than a light hissing, like air being drawn through clenched teeth and yet I sense no one about.

Creeping from my room, I leave the door ajar so as not to make any sound that would alert my friends. I am determined to end this game and even one misstep could spell trouble. No one had been sleeping well in the wake of so much death, and so I'd chosen tonight to use the barbiturates that I carried with me. I slipped them into their tea, and watched as the Sandman lead them off to their dreams. So much the better.

The stone is cold on my bare feet, the soles recoil and it makes my calves cramp painfully. A groan involuntarily escapes my lips, nearly inaudible but not enough for me not to hesitate breathlessly as I listened for stirrings. "Moira?" a breathless voice whispered from nearby. I knew it was too good to be true, and I glance back down the hall to see Jodee standing in the shadows of her doorway. "I didn't mean to Moira. I didn't – I tried not to but I couldn't help it!" her high-pitched hysterical tone rasps off the walls in the mostly empty building.

Echoes in the halls of hell. "What Jodee? What didn't you mean to do," I calmly respond; it crosses my mind to run back into my room and lock it behind me, but instead I stand and watch her step from the darkness in her old-fashioned white nightgown. I used to be white, but now its front is nearly glowing red with gore. "Jodee. Oh what did you do?!" I run to her, mindful of the serrated blade she still holds in her lax grip. There is a drop of blood, shiny as new paint resting pregnant on its tip.

"Jodee, What the hell?!" It was meant to be a scream, it felt like a scream, but it didn't roar. It only turns into a harsh croak. My stomach threatens empty itself as she coughs, spraying my face with gore and then gasps. A wet splattering sound invades the silence and along with it, a thick smell of feces and copper makes me gag. A spill of thick ropy tubes lays on her bare feet, the glow-in-the-dark nail polish on her toes gleams nauseatingly in the darkness.

"She told me to. She. She made me and I didn't believe you and I'm sorry. I'm so fucking sorry."

"Where did you get the knife?" I ask as gently as I am able, horrified to see the colour draining from her face so quickly. Jodee stares at her feet and begins to cry in a frightened childlike way, before sobbing, "She brought the knife, it was on the dresser when I came out of the shower. She made me get dressed and then she held my hand and she made me do this. I couldn't even scream, Moira, that bitch, she took that too," Jodee rasps, placing her cold hand on my cheek, and the other on my shoulder. I can feel the chill from her dying body through my nightgown, a cold dead chill. Jesus. "Moira, you can't stop her. Stop trying, Oh..."

She hunches over, gagging then coughing up a mouthful of thick soup and loose tissue with a liquidy ratcheting sound before craning her neck at an impossible angle, and smiling up at me. I felt myself recoil, disgusted by the blood in her teeth as much as the helpless rictus of that smile. Nearly mechanically she stands upright again, and violently shoves me away. I watch as her hand lifts, and the blade's point glistening with rubies points at my heart. That unholy bitch.

Watch and learn, my daughter

Satan's Whore, she stands just behind Jodee, holding the hand of my friend in her bony fingers so tight that it turns Jodee's skin white. "Stop it! Leave her alone. She's dead already, can't you let her die in peace!" I scream at her, watching in horror as she turns the blade so that it stares Jodee straight in the face. "Moira," Jodee whimpers, "please. Help." I have no time to blink before the blade is driven straight into her eye, skewering the brain beyond. This time her screams are not stolen.

Shriek after shriek peals from her throat as her fist twists the blade deeper. I can hear the metal grinding against the bone, scraping under the endless shrieks and am unable to look away. "***Stop***! Please stop...." My voice cracks, unable to watch the uncontrolled jittering of Jodee's body any further but can't look away or block out the sound of her feet tapping on the floor. Her fingers clench and relax, clench and relax, on and on while the incessant noise of the Lackey's laughter fills my ears. Eric bolts into the hallway from our room, slamming into me and knocking me to the floor, before standing with his mouth agape at Jodee. Her arm gives a mighty yank and removes the blade from the now spurting hole where her eye once lived. Her remaining eye rolls inward, and finally, her body crumbles bonelessly, dead, to the floor.

The Lackey lounges across the hall in the doorway to the stairs I had intended to use to end this insanity, picking at his nails nonchalantly. His smile boils and bubbles with maggots, causing a miasma in the remaining flesh. I can nearly see. the lady of the house crouching in front of me, her madness capers in her eyes. *Elinor*, her insanity gloats in my head, *I am Elinor, Queen.* She drags her fingernails deeply into my cheek, ending my delusions that any of us would get out of here with our lives. My skin crawls and howls, sobbing from the newly dug furrows that are oozing blood in rivulets down my face.

Queen Bitch gives me a coldly cursory glance then regards her bony fingers with interest. I close my eyes, trying to block her from my sight but she is inside my head, painting the hallways and neuropathways with my own blood. The landscapes she creates are against my very nature and I rebel against it, forcibly pushing back from her. The demented cackle hurts my ears; rage hurtling through my veins that is not mine forces me to stand, but I own it.

When I open my lids, she is attempting to wipe Jodee's blood on Eric's lips then, even as he balked, tries to lick his cheek with her blackened tongue. The strength that had receded out of fear and hopelessness rears with its claws bared. She'd taken him away from me, further into the shadows, and had locked him in her putrescent embrace.

"*Get away from him, you corrupt cunt.* He's mine and I've had quite enough of you." Her head whips around, and for a moment I see her as she truly is; a ghost of an echo, nothing more than an airy scent to mask the cloud of rot and decay that follow her appearances. Maybe once she was handsome enough but now Elinor was nothing more than a wet and putrid fragrance that paraded as a flower.

He stands in the way of your destiny
"Your glamour won't work on me anymore Lady Elinor." She bares her teeth at me,

holding Eric closer."That's right, I know your name. I. See. You. He does not, and nor does he stands in my way, only you do and your servant do. To be less than eloquent, fuck off," I spit at her through clenched teeth. Lackey gasps at my words, his rotted disguise appears at his Mistress's feet. He is little more than a spoiled fleshsuit and skitters away from the ineffective kick leveled at him from her pointed slipper.

He stares at her resentfully as she opens her mouth to speak, and I find myself unwilling to hear a single word of her lies. Without a hesitation, I stride forward and clasp Eric's hand in mine, pulling him to the stairwell that leads to the stone walk above, and force him to begin climbing. The spirits are back, each one a glow in the dimness, each smile or caress of is otherworldly gentleness and a salve on my aching body.

Hurry, they urge us, *it's coming*, and we quicken our steps. "Moira," Eric huffs as I push past him and hurry ahead, "Moira, please can't we talk about – "

"No. Keep climbing." The world shudders as her screams assault my senses. They are the wails of a million lost souls, and would be beautiful except the high-pitched screeches and lugubrious tones caught in an onslaught keep it from being remotely close. Eric's warm hand is on my shoulder, and I glance over my shoulder to see his lips moving, and not a word could I hear. Only the rushing of the wind, and the inaudible humming as my third eye vibrates in my mind. I can See again; my abilities have come rushing back and they hit like a freight train. Hard enough that I teeter on the edge, my balance thrown off by the barrage and feel

Eric's warm arms catch me as I falter. He always catches me and I will miss that. "Let's go back to the room," Eric says, brushing the stray lock of hair that has fallen across my face away with his hand, and I stiffen in his arms. The lesser of the two evils is to continue with my plan, through it grieves me to do it and so much less suffering for both of us than what I know will happen if I don't.

"Hurry Eric, let's get out of this place. It'll be better up there," I whisper with my forehead against his chest, lingering in the safety that I'd know that I will miss forever. Pulling back and placing my hand on his cheek, I turn and begin to climb with my eyes burning with unfallen tears. Soon enough this never-ending sequence of steps would take me to the point of no return, and there would be none, for either of us if I had my way.

"Where are we going Moira? I thought we were leaving?" Eric's voice reverberates on the stone walls, interrupting the encouraging song of those that had been taken, and lost here due to their innocence and loyalty.

The early morning sun shines through the cracks in the slats of the old wooden door at the top of the stair, making it seem the entrance to the Above. Eric gasps in awe behind me and we hesitate for a moment, to catch our breath and to admire the beauty together. My mind's eye wanders around corners, prepared to scream the alarm should my plan be uncovered. So far, my returned abilities have not been gleaned, much to my pleasure.

I push the door open and feel the rising sun's rays on my skin like a warm kiss. The heaviness in my heart eases slightly as I walk to the edge of the walkway where I first glimpsed that raving lunatic. Was it only days ago? So much pain and suffering had occurred here since the King's death, and all at the hands of Lady Elinor. My friends have been lost to her insanity, to her unwillingness to let go. Eric's hand is on my shoulder and I turn, wrapping my arms around him in a tight embrace, loathe to let him go.

He kisses the top of my head with a smile, I can feel the curve against my hair. "I love you too silly girl. Look, there's been some damage up here. Look, some of the stones have fallen from that part of the wall." Eric points to the hole in the ancient stone, and I see a gap sitting at about knee height, and let him go to peer over the edge. It's perfect, almost as though it were planned. Stepping away from the edge, slightly, a smiling Eric moves for his own look, babbling away about structural damage and restorations. Shaking my head, I yank him back with a laugh, "Eric, shut up and kiss me."

"Yessum, as you wish" He pulls me tighter and kisses me soundly enough that I again reconsider a return to the bedroom, then take a step forwards, forcing him backwards.

He breaks the kiss, to my regret. "Moira, what are you doing?!" His voice is frantic, far away and faint in my ears.

"I'm ending this mess. I love you." He looks at me in horror and disbelieve, and I kiss him again, placing my hand firmly in the middle of his chest. "It's the only way. I'm sorry. I'm so damned sorry." My tears come the only way they can, as a sob in my own chest, and I push him hard.

Eric's arms pinwheel for balance, his feet shuffling in the gritty floor for purchase and then, he is gone. I hear him scream my name, full of anguish and betrayal, and I scream too. His cry is cut off abruptly and I lean my weight on my hands to peer over the ledge. His body quivers, legs dancing and arms flailing from the top of the spiked fence that surrounds the tiny graveyard that sits beside the castle gardens. His blood splatters the gravestones, and the well maintained lawn underneath him, and he struggles and writhes, alive while I stand here watching.

I'm a monster. I turn to run, fly a fast as my feet will carry me, desperate to reach him so that he wouldn't' have to die alone. Maybe I can take it back. Maybe he will forgive me. But she is there, the Queen of Nothing and her image flashes, fashes my eyes; beauty and bones, rot and roses, over and over and she cries as she snarls. I hate her.

This is your home, Moira.
This is where you belong.

". Were you always insane?" Never in life will I call this home, Elinor. Not when you would destroy everything I care about." I back to the broken ledge, the very same one I'd pushed Eric from moments before, and smile at the sad creature that Elinor truly is. " You lose, Go to Hell, El. You've taken your last life," I show her my middle fingers, step backwards and fall. I can see her at the ledge, hear and feel her enormous shriek of rage. It's a small sacrifice for a larger victory.

"Eric, wait for me. I'm coming," I whisper, closing my eyes and preparing for the punctures my body was about to endure. If death is truly only the start, I am ready to begin the next adventure.

THE SELKIRK SEVEN
THE WAY IT ENDED

I am often drawn back to that moment in the air beyond the ledge. That millisecond spent worrying about whether the slight push I gave as I began my descent would be the difference between being a mouldering corpse six feet down, or left doomed to live in an endless Hell. I awoke into the latter. I landed on the same graveyard fence that Eric had, though death didn't come to me as it had for him. According to the medical examiner's report, he died instantly after landing sideways, breaking his back.

Did I survive?

That is a question that still requires study and therapy; sadly, I am still no closer to a resolution. I suppose that the answer depends on your definition of survival. I am alive; my body functions as does my chest and right leg healed slowly, limped along, as it were. The holes in my body healed slowly and with a lot of anguish, physical and emotional. So did the broken bones. I can walk short distances now, alone instead of with any number of chatty chaperones. I eat and drink, and sometimes, I sleep without nightmares. I speak to people, socialize and smile as though I hadn't died and have no history of tragedy or trauma.

It's amazing how far a mask of confidence can carry you. But there are two people I never have to wear that mask for. One of them is Jake Jepson. Out of the seven, only Jake Jepson and I made it out. Mr. James had been pulling up in his Bentley and witnessed my decent and subsequent landing.

According to Jake, instead of calling for help, he fell to his knees wailing his loyalty and was still pleading for forgiveness from his failures when the ambulance pulled into the drive. Jake told the authorities that he kicked Mr. James in the ribs and made the call that saved my life on his cellular phone. The recorded call from emergency services confirms that Mr. James was indeed calling out for mercy and his culpability. They arrested him and found him guilty of first degree murder in the deaths of Eric Dupree, Jodee Dean, Charley Fargo, Mark Conrad and Logan Roofe

Jake and I should have been numbered among them and I know that we are both still haunted by the visions of our friends and loved ones. We stayed in touch for a while, out of survivor's guilt more than anything I suppose. It eventually came to the point where it was just too painful to try. I still hear from him at Christmas and on the anniversary, without fail.

They found Walter Henry James of Selkirk and New Leithshire dead in his cell 8 months into his life sentence, scalped and missing his heart. They have no leads nor are they looking for answers. I suppose one could consider it a just dessert for a man who lived to steal the lives of others.

As for me, my main regret is that I didn't have the opportunity to tell Eric something very important, something that might have changed his final moments, and made them happy instead of devastated. In the meantime, miracles happen

My miracle came into the world at 3:13 pm on October 17, 2015. Her name is Joely Erica Dupree, and she resembles her daddy as though she were a clone. There is nothing I love more than looking into her sweet little face and seeing his smile every single day. It's almost like having him back again.

Jacob Jepson is her godfather and he loves her as though she were his own. Joely couldn't want for a more attentive male role model in her life. The doctors are stumped as to how she clung to life during all the physical trauma but I know how. She is a gift, a treasure from her father that I cherish beyond my own life. Joely is the one good thing that came of our experiences at Selkirk Keep.

He video chatted with us today, after calling to say that he needed to see Joely. It was an odd thing for him say, the way he said it and his voice sounded strange. I'm concerned about his state of mind. During our conversation and while reminiscing, Joely started to cry, fussing when she usually is excited to see him. He called her Elinor and said that the bloodline is secure.

Oh Eric, I'm afraid for our daughter.

ABOUT THE AUTHOR

I am a Canadian based writer who resides in Calgary, Alberta and am a Warrior Mom blessed with two challenging boys, Sam 14 and Davey 10. I am a rabid supporter of Independent Film and Publications, and a horror junkie with a taste for words, and bloodsauce. Most recently, I was voice talent to The Carmen Theatre Group as Maria Sanchez and I can be seen in The Orphan Killer 2: Bound x Blood, written and created by Matt Farnsworth.

SLAYFUL FRIENDS

THESE PEOPLE ARE TALENTED AND WONDERFUL FRIENDS. PLEASE TAKE THE TIME TO VISIT THEIR SITES AND SUPPORT INDEPENDENT ARTISTS AND AUTHORS.

THANK YOU XO

MORBIDX ALTERNATIVE MODELING
FACEBOOK @MORBIDXALTMODELING

THOMAS DUDER - THE AUTHOR OF THINGS
THEPENISMYSWORD.COM

CRASHPALACE PRODUCTIONS
CRASHPALACEPRODUCTIONS.COM

THE CARMEN THEATRE GROUP
CARMENTHEATERONLINE.COM

BLAZING OWL PRESS
BLAZINGOWLPRESS.COM

HGB ENTERTAINMENT LTD.
HGBFILMS.CA

SMACKTONGUE INDEPENDENT RADIO WITH MICHAEL LANE
SMACKTONGUE.COM

THY DEMONS BE SCRIBBLIN'
THYDEMONSBESCRIBBLIN.COM

TIM MILLER – EXTREME HORROR AUTHOR
TIMMILLER.ORG

Made in the USA
Lexington, KY
21 May 2019